W9-BWF-518

THE LIBRARY BUS

BY **Bahram Rahman**

ILLUSTRATED BY
Gabrielle Grimard

pajamapress

First published in Canada and the United States in 2020

Text copyright © 2020 Bahram Rahman
Illustration copyright © 2020 Gabrielle Grimard
This edition copyright © 2020 Pajama Press Inc.
This is a first edition.

10 9 8 7 6 5 4 3 2 1

All rights reserved. No part of this publication may be reproduced, stored in a retrieval system or
transmitted, in any form or by any means, without the prior written consent of the publisher or a licence
from The Canadian Copyright Licensing Agency (Access Copyright). For an Access Copyright licence,
visit www.accesscopyright.ca or call toll free 1.800.893.5777.

www.pajamapress.ca   info@pajamapress.ca

 Canada Council Conseil des arts
for the Arts   du Canada
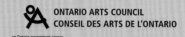 ONTARIO ARTS COUNCIL
CONSEIL DES ARTS DE L'ONTARIO
an Ontario government agency
un organisme du gouvernement de l'Ontario
 Canadä

The publisher gratefully acknowledges the support of the Canada Council for the Arts and the Ontario
Arts Council for its publishing program. We acknowledge the financial support of the Government of
Canada through the Canada Book Fund (CBF) for our publishing activities.

Library and Archives Canada Cataloguing in Publication

Title: The library bus / by Bahram Rahman ; illustrated by Gabrielle Grimard.
Names: Rahman, Bahram, 1984- author. | Grimard, Gabrielle, illustrator.
Identifiers: Canadiana 20200203533 | ISBN 9781772781014 (hardcover)
Subjects: LCGFT: Picture books.
Classification: LCC PS8635.A36 L53 2020 | DDC jC813/.6—dc23

Publisher Cataloging-in-Publication Data (U.S.)
Names: Rahman, Bahram, 1984-, author. | Grimard, Gabrielle, 1975-,
    illustrator.
Title: The Library Bus / by Bahram Rahman; illustrated by Gabrielle Grimard.
Description: Toronto, Ontario Canada : Pajama Press, 2020. | Summary: "Five-year-old Pari accompanies
her mother on her library bus rounds for the first time, stopping at a village and a refugee camp so that
girls there can exchange books and have a lesson in English. Talking with her mother as they drive, Pari
learns that she is lucky that she can attend school the next year. Pari's mother had to learn in secret when
it was forbidden to teach girls to read, and the young women the bus visits weekly have no other access
to education. Inspired by the first library bus to operate in Kabul, Afghanistan" -- Provided by publisher.
Identifiers: ISBN 978-1-77278-101-4 (hardcover)
Subjects: LCSH: Books and reading – Juvenile fiction. | Refugees -- Juvenile fiction. | Libraries – Juvenile
fiction. | BISAC: JUVENILE FICTION / Books & Libraries. | JUVENILE FICTION / People & Places /
Middle East. | JUVENILE FICTION / Social Themes / Homelessness & Poverty.
Classification: LCC PZ7.1R346Li |DDC [E] – dc23

Original art created with watercolor and digital media
Cover and book design—Rebecca Bender

Printed in China by Qualibre Inc.

Pajama Press Inc.
181 Carlaw Ave. Suite 251 Toronto, Ontario Canada, M4M 2S1

Distributed in Canada by UTP Distribution
5201 Dufferin Street Toronto, Ontario Canada, M3H 5T8

Distributed in the U.S. by Ingram Publisher Services
1 Ingram Blvd. La Vergne, TN 37086, USA

For my mother *jan*

—B.R.

To all the beautiful people who
contribute in their own way
to make the world a better place

—G.G.

"Arrange the books...clean up...be nice to the other girls," Pari repeats under her breath.

"You'll be great," Mama says, giving Pari a hug.

Today is Pari's first day as Mama's library helper. But this is no ordinary library—this one is on wheels! And it's the only library bus in all of Kabul. Instead of seats, it has so many books that Pari can barely count them all.

The streets are still dark when Pari and Mama leave home.
Their first stop is a small village tucked in a valley between two
gray mountains. A fiery sun rises over the passing fields.

A group of girls stands under a
giant oak tree, waiting patiently.

One little girl waves her chador.
"Over here," she shouts.

Pari opens the back door, and everyone climbs inside. The girls return the books they borrowed last week and search through the shelves for new books to read.

"*Sallam*, my girls…let's make a circle now," Mama says in a calm voice. Everyone pays attention. "We are going to practice some English."

First, they sing the alphabet song.
Then they count from one to ten.

When the lesson ends, a girl in a yellow dress skips over to
Pari. "Are you new here?" she asks. "What's your name? Do
you live here on the bus? Can you print A, B, C? I can print
the letters all the way to Z." She talks very fast.

"I can print them too," Pari says
quickly. But Pari can't even read
or write in Farsi yet.

Mama starts the bus—*Bwob-b-b...Vroom!*—and they are off to a refugee camp beyond the mountains. The old city spreads out in front of them like the colorful embroidered scarfs in the Grand Bazaar. Tiny houses, dusty roads, one hill after another, and then a ring of rugged mountains.

Pari fidgets with her zipper. "When did you learn A, C, D, Mama?" she asks.

"Oh, you mean, A, B, C. That's the English alphabet, just like *Alif, Be, Te* in Farsi."

Mama takes a deep breath. "Grandpa taught me a long time ago. When I was young, girls were not allowed to go to school, to learn to read or write. I had to hide in the basement to study."

Pari wonders if Mama was ever afraid in Grandpa's
basement. It is always dark down there.

"Pari, when you go to school next year, I want you to study hard. Never stop learning. Then you will be free. Tell me now," she adds with a wink, "how does learning make you feel?"

"Free!"

Pari screams,
raising her
arms in the air.

It is midday when they arrive at the camp. Pari sees rows and rows of tents. There is dust everywhere and the kids have patches on their clothes.

Mama announces, "Those who need notebooks and pencils, go to Pari. And those exchanging books, come to me."

Pari is surrounded by a crowd of girls asking for school supplies.

"I need a new pencil," a curly-haired girl shouts.

Another girl squeezes her way to the front of the line. "Give me a notebook," she says, jumping up and down with excitement.

Soon everyone is ready for a lesson. "A, B, C, D…repeat after me. One more time." Mama makes it sound like a beautiful song.

"A, B, C…" Pari sings to herself. Very softly.

As they leave the camp, Pari reads the large letters written on the tents. "W...F...P, and the next one is

U
  N
    H
      C
        R."

"Good job, Pari!" Mama cries. "You got them right."

Pari beams with pride.

Back at home, Pari helps Mama make dinner—a bowl of hearty bean *shorba* with chunks of potato and carrot. At the table she asks, "Next year, will you teach me to read?"

Mama says, "You will go to a real school in the city."

"Why can't those girls go to a real school too?" Pari asks.

"There are no schools for girls in the village or the camp. They only have the library bus once a week. But I will help them the same way your grandpa helped me."

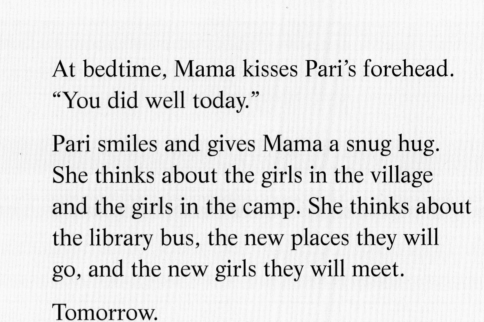

At bedtime, Mama kisses Pari's forehead.
"You did well today."

Pari smiles and gives Mama a snug hug.
She thinks about the girls in the village
and the girls in the camp. She thinks about
the library bus, the new places they will
go, and the new girls they will meet.

Tomorrow.

A NOTE ABOUT REFUGEE CAMPS

When war, famine, or a natural disaster forces large numbers of people to leave their homes, many end up living in refugee camps. These camps have only basic shelters, usually tents. The people who live there don't have access to normal ways of getting work, food, or schooling.

The letters Pari reads on the tents at the refugee camp are the names of two organizations that help people in these conditions. The World Food Programme (WFP) provides food to displaced people. The United Nations High Commissioner for Refugees (UNHCR) protects them. The UNHCR also helps displaced people to return home once it's safe, or to begin the long process of finding a new country to settle in.

You might wonder what it was like to grow up in Afghanistan.

If I tell you that my childhood was "okay," you might think I am joking. Afghanistan has experienced war and human suffering for many years. How could anyone's life there be okay?

What I am saying is that when you are born in war, you are truly unaware of the alternative, peace. War is your normal. Yet still life carries on, no matter how long or short your time may be. You go to school or learn at home. You play with your friends. You laugh and cry. You get hurt and heal. And you dream. Big dreams like those of every other child on the planet.

I wrote *The Library Bus* to tell you that story. The story of strength shown by children in Afghanistan, in particular Afghan girls, in pursuit of education. I also wanted to celebrate female teachers. They are brave and resourceful. In their creative ways, they make it possible for girls to continue their education in spite of many obstacles. Teachers run mobile schools and libraries, provide homeschooling, and so much more.

While I have taken the liberty to rearrange some of the events in this book, all of the characters are inspired by the children that I met during my visits to refugee camps and orphanages in Kabul. They are the real heroes of Afghanistan. I thank each and every one of them from the bottom of my heart.

—Bahram Rahman